RECEIVED
D0475195

Snitchy Witch

by Frank J. Sileo, PhD

illustrated by MacKenzie Haley

MAGINATION PRESS · WASHINGTON, DC
American Psychological Association

To my dearest friend Melanie Rush. A love for the supernatural show Haven *brought us together. Friendship, love, support, and family is our magic potion*—FJS

To my parents; your support and love have been the magic that fuels my art—MH

Magination Press is a registered trademark of the American Psychological Association.
Order books at maginationpress.org, or call 1-800-374-2721.

Book design by Susan K. White

Printed by Worzalla, Stevens Point, WI

Library of Congress Cataloging-in-Publication Data

Names: Sileo, Frank J., 1967– author. | Haley, MacKenzie, illustrator.
Title: Snitchy witch / by Frank J. Sileo, PhD ; illustrated by MacKenzie Haley.
Description: Washington, DC : Magination Press, [2019] | «American Psychological Association.» |
Summary: Wanda's snitching is spoiling the fun at Camp Spellbound, so some of her fellow campers cast a spell to teach her the difference between tattling and telling.
Identifiers: LCCN 2018038337| ISBN 9781433830228 (hardcover) | ISBN 1433830221 (hardcover)
Subjects: | CYAC: Talebearing—Fiction. | Witchcraft—Fiction. | Camps—Fiction. | Behavior—Fiction.
Classification: LCC PZ7.S582 Wan 2019 | DDC [E]—dc23 LC record available at https://lccn.loc.gov/2018038337

Manufactured in the United States of America
10 9 8 7 6 5 4 3 2 1

It was a full moon at Camp Spellbound.

Every year, witches from all over
fly in on their brooms.

It's a hair-raising, fun time.

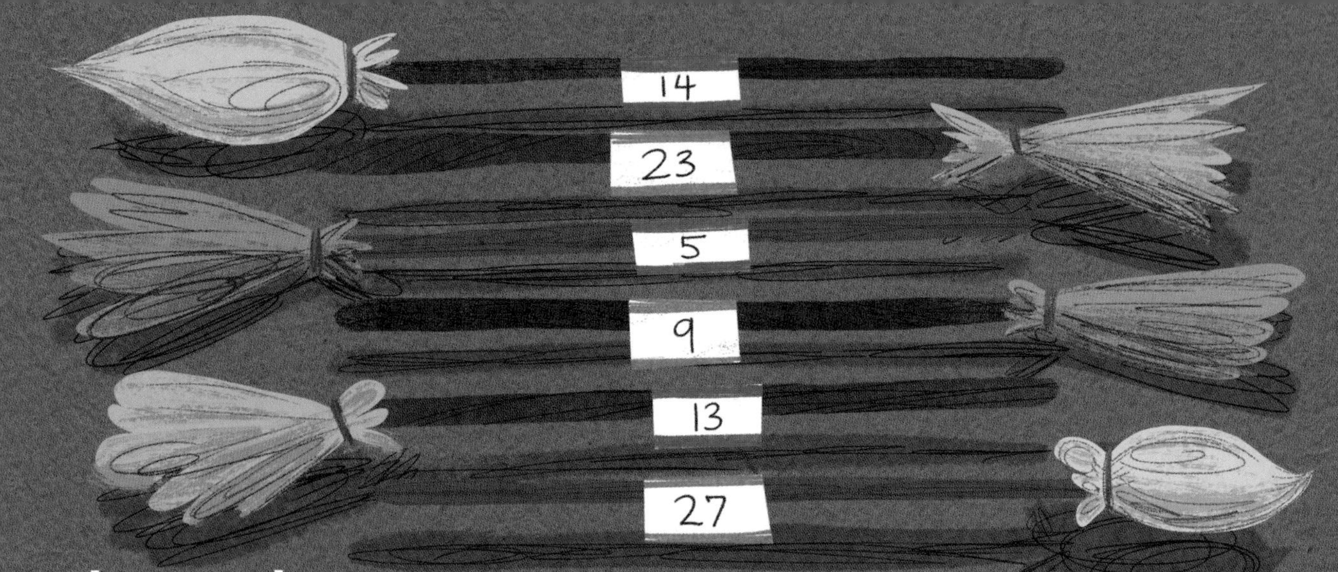

There are broom races.

Magic potion swaps.

Cackling contests.

And hat decorating parties.

But one witch liked to snitch. And this caused trouble.

Wanda liked to get attention from the Head Witch. Whenever Wanda believed someone was doing something wrong, she would tattle on them.

She snitched on William when he took food from the cauldron before dinner.

—Line cutter!

She snitched on Wendy for cutting in line.

Potion Spiller!—

She snitched on Wyatt
for spilling some potion on the floor.

She snitched on Winnie for getting fingerprints on the crystal ball.

She even snitched on Ben the Black Cat for meowing too loud while everyone was sleeping!

The witches were wickedly angry with Wanda for snitching on everyone. Winnie let out a bloodcurdling scream!

No one wanted to spend time with Wanda at camp.

Wanda asked Wyatt why no one was talking to her or playing with her.

"We are angry because you tattle on us just to get us in trouble. That's snitching. It hurts our feelings. You only tell when someone is hurt, could get hurt, or you need help from a grown-up."

Wanda laughed. "That's a hoot! Really!
I'm not a snitch!"
But then she thought about all the times
she told on others.

Later that night, several of the campers met down in the dungeon when no one was around.

Oh moon so full, round, and bright, we beg one favor of you tonight. For witches who tattle, witches who snitch, tie their tongues, zip their lips! No witch shall squeal or tell on friends. This spell will be broken when the snitching ends!

"Let's put a spell on her tongue," William cackled.

"A spell that doesn't allow her to speak! That will teach her a lesson!" Wyatt howled.

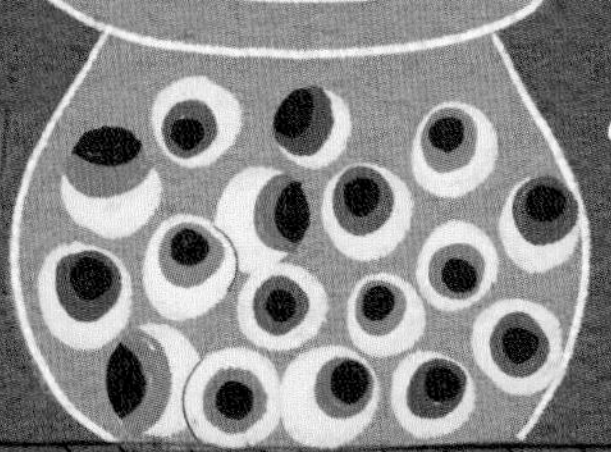

"Sounds chilling!" said Winnie.

They pulled out a big book of spells.

"Here's one on snitching!" Wendy pointed out.

Everyone recited the spell together.

Oh moon so full, round, and bright, we beg one favor of you tonight. For witches who tattle, witches who snitch,

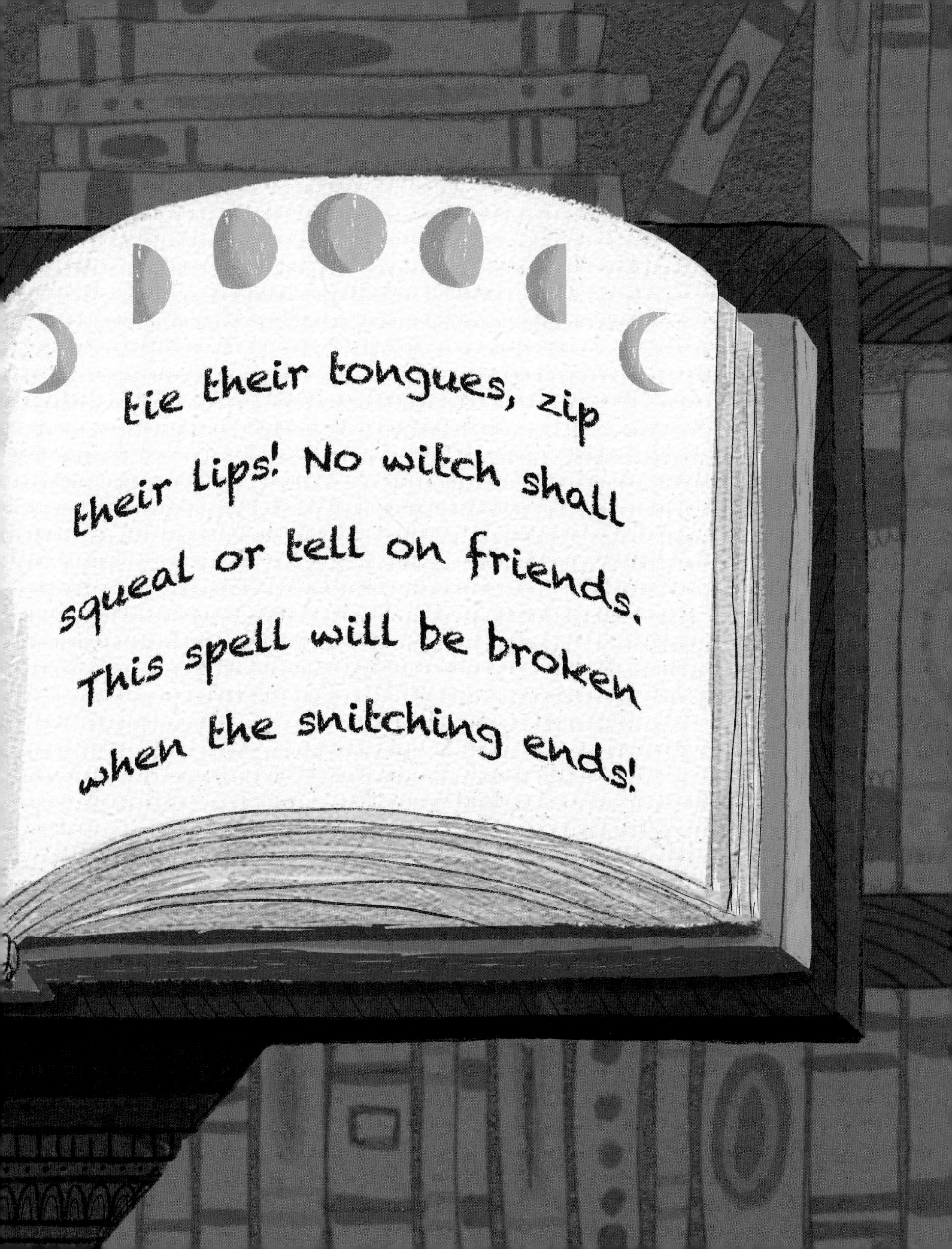

tie their tongues, zip
their lips! No witch shall
squeal or tell on friends.
This spell will be broken
when the snitching ends!

The next morning, Wanda went to greet the others. But when she tried to speak, no words came out of her mouth. "Someone must have cast a spell on me," she thought.

DONUTS

During breakfast, she saw Winnie taking an extra donut. She wanted to tell the Head Witch but her voice was silent.

She saw Wendy take things for a potion that did not belong to her. Again, she tried to tell but nothing came out of her mouth.

Wanda then saw Elmira taking out some of the straw from William's broom.

That could cause the broom to fail during the broom race. William might fall and hurt himself!

Wanda ran to the Head Witch.

She took a deep breath and tried to speak.

She mouthed “Elmira touched William’s broom!” But nothing came out of her mouth. “That sounds like a snitch,” Wanda thought.

Wanda tried to speak again.
"Someone was trying to cheat."
Once again nothing came out of her
mouth. It sounded like a snitch.

Time was running out.
Wanda thought and thought. "I got it!"

"I'm really worried about William."
Her voice was back!
The spell was broken!

"What is it?" asked the Head Witch.

"I'm not snitching! Someone's in trouble!" Wanda said.

"That's right," said the Head Witch.
"Tell me what you are worried about."

Wanda told the Head Witch what she saw.

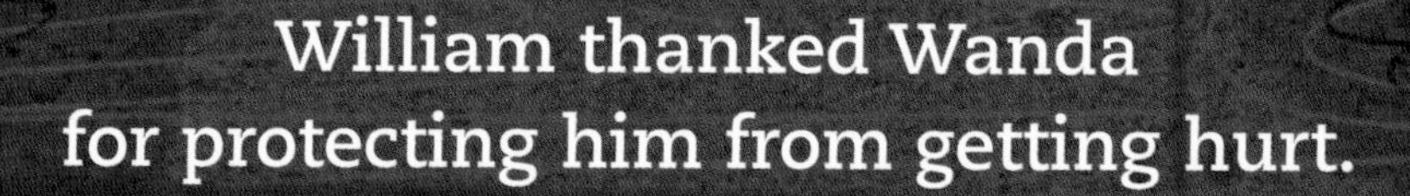

William thanked Wanda
for protecting him from getting hurt.

The witches apologized for casting a spell on her tongue. “We just wanted to help you stop snitching,” said Wendy.

“You don’t need to snitch, Wanda,” said William. “You almost lost your friends because snitching gets people in trouble.”

"From now on, I will zip my lips and
never snitch," Wanda promised.

For the rest of the day,
Wanda and her friends sat
around the cauldron,
cackling it up, and having fun.

Wanda was glad she made the switch
from being a snitch!

Note to Grown-Up Witches

"He won't share his game with me!"
"She won't give me the red crayon!"
"He didn't eat his broccoli!"
"She keeps staring and laughing at me!"

Do some of these statements sound familiar? As a parent, teacher, or caregiver, you may hear statements like these on a daily basis. Snitching or tattling on others is a common behavior among children. As they are growing up, learning about the rules of life, and developing social skills, children may snitch on their siblings, friends, and even grown-ups at home or at school.

As parents and caregivers, we spend a great deal of our time teaching children about rules—*Chew with your mouth closed. Keep your hands to yourself. Share your toys with others. Don't touch things that do not belong to you.* Young children are learning what the rules are, what happens when they break them, and are figuring out right from wrong. They have a strong desire for things to be fair. As they learn the rules at home, school, and socially, it is only natural for children to want to bring attention to behavior they perceive as breaking the rules. *Snitchy Witch* serves as a tool for parents and caregivers to open up a discussion about when it is important to say something to an adult, and when and how children can work things out on their own.

Snitching Versus Telling

Snitching or *tattling* is telling on someone when the situation is safe and does not require an adult to be involved. There are various reasons why children engage in this behavior:

- to get someone in trouble. Most of the time snitching is harmless but sometimes a child wants to hurt another child in a non-physical way;
- to gain attention from adults;
- to be noticed;
- because they feel left out by others;
- to try to please a parent, teacher, or other caregiver;
- to get someone to stop doing something that annoys them;
- to show that they know the rules. Children may believe they will be rewarded for not engaging in bad behavior like their siblings or peers. We read this in the story where Wanda Witch told on some of the witches to get them in trouble or to get attention from the Head Witch;
- because of feelings of jealousy;
- to gain power over a sibling or peer;
- because of a strong desire to be in charge; *and*
- because young children tend to be concrete in their thinking. They may not yet have developed the capacity for abstract thinking and advanced reasoning skills. They are rigid about rules and may believe they are doing the right thing by snitching. In addition, young children may not have developed the skills of effective interpersonal problem solving and managing conflicts with others.

There are instances where children should be taught to always tell an adult that something is going on. This is *telling* or *reporting*. A child should speak up if someone (including themselves) or something is being hurt or is in danger, or when someone is deliberately being destructive or hurtful. Physical and verbal bullying is something children should report whether it is occurring to them or another individual.

Depending on their age, and their cognitive and social developmental stage, it can be difficult for children to differentiate between a situation that is dangerous and one that isn't. It is our job as parents and caregivers to help them understand the difference. Let your child know it's okay to ask you if they are unsure about a situation. (Always check out the situation because you never know if something may be dangerous.)

Talk through situations with your child so they can understand the differences between snitching and telling. Give concrete examples, such as:

Snitching: "He cut in line at the water fountain!"
Telling: "He pushed me and punched me to get to the water fountain!"

In the first example, explain to your child that cutting in line, although it is not polite, did not create an unsafe situation. In the second example, discuss how pushing and punching is a behavior that should be told to an adult because it involves someone getting hurt and would be best resolved by a grown-up.

What Can You Do When Your Child Snitches?

Teaching your child the difference between *snitching* and *telling* is a great starting point. Children have learned to go to the grown-ups in their lives to have their needs met and to solve problems. With time, practice, and patience, children can learn when telling an adult is necessary, and when they can handle problems on their own. The following are some guidelines for addressing snitching and encouraging children to solve problems on their own.

Teach problem-solving skills. Telling children "Go work it out" is not an effective approach to this issue because children may not have learned the tools for dealing with conflict and problems. On the other hand, if we step in too often and too quickly it teaches our children that the only way to solve problems is for adults to handle them. Help your child problem-solve how to work through conflicts with others with your guidance. Encourage your child to take several breaths and think about a way to handle the situation before tattling. Ask them, "What do you think would be the best way to make this better?" Help your child by giving them the tools to solve problems; suggest using words ("I don't like when you don't share with me") or walking away and playing with someone or something else.

For example, if the problem centers on sharing with a peer or sibling, encourage them to negotiate with others and take turns.

Examples could be:
"Why don't you take turns playing the videogame? Maybe we can do rock-paper-scissors to see who goes first."
"What else can you play with that you will both be happy with?"

As children grow and mature, their social and problem-solving skills will improve and they will snitch less. When children are encouraged to problem-solve, they will feel more confident in their ability to handle difficult, frustrating situations. When they improve their independent problem-solving skills, children will be less likely to run to you each and every time a problem arises and snitching will decrease.

Avoid rewarding the behavior. Remember that children may snitch to get attention from an adult. You do not always have to jump in right away when your child snitches. There may be a tendency on your part to scold or punish the alleged "perpetrator." When you do this you are rewarding the snitching behavior. It gives the "snitcher" a false sense of importance and you will encounter more snitching behaviors. There are times when you do need to step in when someone is getting hurt or when there are safety issues. When safety is not an issue, do not punish the other child as it will reward and reinforce the snitching. You want to avoid giving